W9-CHM-112

True Colors

Also by Jill Santopolo

Sparkle Spa

Book 1: All That Glitters

Book 2: Purple Nails
and Puppy Tails

Book 3: Makeover Magic

Coming Soon

Book 5: Bad News Nails

✳ · ✳ · ✳ · ✳

Book 4
True Colors

JILL SANTOPOLO

Aladdin
NEW YORK   LONDON   TORONTO   SYDNEY   NEW DELHI

🪔ALADDIN
An imprint of Simon & Schuster Children's Publishing Division
1230 Avenue of the Americas, New York, NY 10020
This Aladdin hardcover edition October 2014
Text copyright © 2014 by Simon & Schuster, Inc.
Jacket illustrations and interior spot illustrations copyright © 2014 by Cathi Mingus
All rights reserved, including the right of reproduction in whole or in part in any form.
ALADDIN is a trademark of Simon & Schuster, Inc., and related logo is
a registered trademark of Simon & Schuster, Inc.
Also available in an Aladdin paperback edition.
For information about special discounts for bulk purchases, please contact
Simon & Schuster Special Sales at 1-866-506-1949 or business@simonandschuster.com.
The Simon & Schuster Speakers Bureau can bring authors to your live event. For more
information or to book an event, contact the Simon & Schuster Speakers Bureau
at 1-866-248-3049 or visit our website at www.simonspeakers.com.
Series designed by Jeanine Henderson
Jacket designed by Karin Paprocki
The text of this book was set in Adobe Caslon.
Manufactured in the United States of America 0814 FFG
10 9 8 7 6 5 4 3 2 1
Library of Congress Control Number 2014933120
ISBN 978-1-4424-7390-4 (hc)
ISBN 978-1-4424-7389-8 (pbk)
ISBN 978-1-4424-7391-1 (eBook)

For my dazzling agent, Miriam Altshuler

With gobs of glittery thank-yous to editrix extraordinaire Karen Nagel and my team of sparkly writer friends, especially Eliot Schrefer, who read this one for me super quickly and gave me wonderfully helpful feedback

Contents

True Colors

✳ ✳ ✳ ✳

one

Not-So-Mellow Yellow

G ive that back!" Brooke Tanner yelled as she chased her puppy around the living room couch and underneath the leaves of a rubber plant. "Sparkly, I mean it!"

But Sparkly didn't listen. With Brooke's glittery Not-So-Mellow Yellow–colored hair band hanging out of his tiny mouth, the puppy raced up the steps and then back down. Brooke was at his heels.

"Sparkly, stop!" Brooke shouted. "Now! Stop!"

"Maybe if you stopped chasing him, he'd stop

running!" Aly Tanner called from the kitchen. It was early Tuesday morning, and Aly was preparing two bowls of cereal for breakfast: a purple bowl for herself, and a pink one for her younger sister, Brooke. Both bowls had granola inside. And blueberries.

"But I want my hair band!" Brooke shouted back to her sister.

"Like I said, if you want it back, just stop running!" Aly yelled into the living room.

"But what if he eats it when I stop?" Brooke sped into the kitchen after Sparkly, who leapt over the girls' backpacks. Brooke leapt over them too, but her sneaker caught in her backpack strap and—*bam!*—she crashed to the ground.

"Ow!" she screamed. "Ow! Ow! Ow!"

Aly went running over. For a minute she wondered if Brooke was fine and just being dramatic, which was the case with Brooke a lot of the time. But tears were running down Brooke's cheeks, and she was holding her arm against her stomach.

"I heard it crack, Aly," she sobbed. "Get Mom."

Now it was Aly's turn to race through the house, ducking under the leaves of the rubber plant, flying around furniture and then up the stairs until she got to their parents' bathroom.

"Brooke fell! She thinks her arm is broken!" Aly pounded on the door, yelling over the sound of a hair dryer.

"What did you say, sweetie?" the girls' mom asked as she cracked open the door.

Aly repeated herself, and then Mom took off, racing down the steps two at a time, Aly right behind her. When they reached the kitchen, Brooke was right where Aly had left her, still on the floor, still crying. Sparkly was whining and nudging Brooke's hair band toward her.

"That won't help anymore, Sparkly!" Brooke whimpered through her tears.

Mom bent down, asked Brooke a few questions, touched her arm in a few spots—which made Brooke yell even louder—and then said to Aly, "I have to take your sister to the hospital. Please call Joan and tell her what happened. She'll have to take you to school today."

As much as Aly liked spending time with Joan—who was the girls' favorite manicurist at their mom's salon, True Colors—she didn't like this plan at all. What if something was *really* wrong with Brooke? What if Brooke needed her? Aly couldn't go to school. She had to be there for Brooke. The sisters were a team.

"Can't I come with you and Brooke?" she asked. "To make her feel better?"

Mom shook her head. "Sorry, Aly," she said. "I don't know what's going to happen at the hospital or how long it'll take. You can go straight to the salon after school. Either I'll be there or Joan will fill you in. You have her number, right?"

Aly nodded. "It's on the refrigerator, just like it always is."

Brooke wasn't crying as hard now, which made Aly feel a little bit better about leaving her. But not all better about it.

Mom ran her hand through her hair, which she hadn't finished drying, and twisted it into a messy bun. "It's times like these that I wish your father didn't travel all week long."

"Do you think he'll come home early?" Brooke asked, sniffling, as Mom carefully helped her up off the floor.

"Let's call him from the car," Mom said.

Once Mom pulled the door shut behind her, Aly called Joan. And when she started explaining what happened, she found herself crying a little.

"I bet that was scary," Joan said.

"It was," Aly said, crying a little more now. "And what if Brooke's really hurt?"

"If Brooke's hurt, the doctors will make her better," Joan said. "Now sit tight, and I'll be right there to take you to school. Get Sparkly's leash on too, so I can bring him to the salon."

All day long Aly worried about Brooke. She had trouble paying attention in class. She kept looking at her purple polka-dot watch to see if it was 3:07 yet, the end of the school day, when she could go to True Colors and find out if her sister was okay. But every time she checked, it wasn't even close to 3:07. Time was moving slower than the snail that Aly and Brooke had watched crawl across the sidewalk the weekend before.

At lunchtime Aly sat with her two best friends, Charlotte and Lily, as usual, but she was too distracted to concentrate on their conversation about the Lewis and Clark project that was due next Monday. She sat, barely touching her bagel and cream cheese, barely even drinking her orange juice, until Lily asked if there were any open appointments left at Sparkle Spa that afternoon.

"Umm," Aly said, "I don't know if we'll even open today."

"But it's Tuesday," Charlotte said. "You're *always* open on Tuesdays for the soccer team's rainbow sparkle pedicures."

Aly clapped a hand over her mouth. "Oh no!" she said. "You're right. It's Tuesday! And Brooke won't be there! And the whole soccer team is coming! And they're going to be in the quarterfinals this weekend! And they're going to be in the quarterfinals this weekend! This is going to be a disaster."

Sparkle Spa

Sparkle Spa was a business that Aly and Brooke started in the back room of their mom's nail salon. Kids could have their nails and toes polished and not take up time or space in the busy grown-up salon. Plus, it was more fun when it was just kids. They could pretty much do whatever they wanted, and as long as they were quiet, no one really bothered them.

It was because of the soccer team—the Auden Angels—that the spa had started in the first place. Their captain, Jenica Posner, came to True Colors one day, and Aly—not an actual salon manicurist— wound up giving Jenica a rainbow sparkle pedicure. Brooke had come up with the color combination, and Jenica thought it was really cool.

Jenica scored so many goals in the next soccer game that the whole team wanted rainbow sparkle pedicures too. And they still came every week so that their "sparkle power" wouldn't fade. So far, they were undefeated for the season and had made it all the way to the quarterfinals.

The team insisted it was due to the sparkles. Aly was pretty sure it was because they were awesome soccer players, but she couldn't risk not giving them sparkle power before the quarterfinals, just in case. Even with Brooke gone, Aly would *have* to do the Angels' pedicures this afternoon. She didn't want it to be her fault if they lost this week. But how would she give all those sparkle pedicures without Brooke's help?

Maybe if I make a list, I can figure it out, Aly thought.

Making lists was something Aly did to organize her thoughts and help her solve problems.

She took a sheet of paper from her notebook and began writing.

Ways to Make Sure All the Angels
Get Their Sparkle Power

1. Walk to True Colors as fast as
   possible.
2. Ask Jenica if some players can
   come on other days.
3. Find more manicurists.

Aly stopped writing and looked up at Charlotte
and Lily.

"I know this is a ridiculous question, but is there
any chance either one of you learned how to polish
nails over the weekend?" Aly asked her friends.

Both girls shook their heads. "Sorry, Aly," Lily said.

"But we can help with other things!" Charlotte
offered.

"Absolutely," Lily agreed. "We'll both come with
you after school."

"I guess that's better than nothing," Aly said, taking a bite of her bagel, even though she was feeling kind of sick to her stomach. "Thanks."

She started to think of a fourth item for her list when she heard, "Is it really, really true that Brooke broke her arm?"

Aly turned. It was Brooke's best friend, Sophie, who had just come in from recess. Her face was flushed, and her dark bangs stuck to her forehead.

"Hi, Soph. I won't know about Brooke until later. Do you want to come with us to Sparkle Spa after school and find out?"

"Please, can I?" Sophie begged. "I'll call my mom from there, if that's all right." She looked as anxious as Aly felt.

"You can help with the soccer team's pedicures, if you want," Charlotte added. "Even if you can't polish."

Sophie's eyes lit up. "I'd be happy to. Anything for Brooke. And for the Sparkle Spa."

The bell rang for class, and as the girls walked together down the hall, Aly thought, *Well, that's three helpers. But not even three people will equal one Brooke.*

two

Red Between the Lines

On the way to True Colors after school, Aly taught Charlotte, Lily, and Sophie how to racewalk. When Aly and Brooke wanted to get somewhere fast and didn't want to—or weren't allowed to—run, they racewalked. It involved lifting your knees high to take very big steps and swinging your elbows to move forward. There was a man in town who had been a racewalker in the Olympics, and Aly and Brooke had learned by copying him.

Aly wondered if Brooke would've gotten hurt if she'd been racewalking around the house this morning instead of running. But then again, Sparkly had been zipping around so quickly, racewalking wouldn't have been fast enough to catch him anyway.

"Am I doing the elbows right?" Sophie asked while they sped to the salon.

Aly glanced over and checked. "Perfect elbows, Sophie," she said.

Aly saw the light-blue True Colors sign up ahead.

"Thank goodness we're almost there!" she heard Lily say behind her. "This is hard work!"

Aly didn't think so, but she was glad they were close. She was really worried about Brooke. And the sooner they got to the salon, the sooner she could find out how her sister was doing.

When Aly pushed open the door to True Colors, the chimes jangled loudly. She looked around the salon for her mom and sister, but she didn't see either one. Joan was seated at the reception desk, Sparkly snoozing at her feet.

"Aly!" she said, standing up.

"Joan!" Aly said, flying into her arms. "How's Brooke? Where is she? What's happening? Where's my mom?"

Joan gave Aly a squeeze. Sparkly woke up and yipped, and Aly picked him up.

"Brooke's home resting. She broke her arm and has a cast. She's going to need to rest for a few days, and she won't be able to run around for a while, but she'll be good as new before you know it. Your mom is home with her."

"Whew!" Lily said. "I'm glad that's all it is! I had a broken arm once. Remember that time in kindergarten when I fell off the swings and needed a cast for a while?"

Aly nodded. She did remember now, but she hadn't until that moment. "Did it hurt?" she asked, hoping the answer was no.

"A little," Lily said. "At the beginning. And then it was itchy. And heavy. And I had to wear a sling. But it wasn't as bad as breaking a leg and needing crutches. That happened to my mom once, and it was the pits."

"That happened to me once too," Mrs. Bass said from the drying station. She was a True Colors regular and sometimes gave the girls books that once belonged to her sons. "A broken leg is a disaster. But a broken arm isn't that bad. Tell Brooke that having a broken arm is a great excuse to sit in bed with a good book."

"I'll tell her," Aly said, though she thought Brooke was more likely to draw than to read. Brooke was a talented artist, just like their mother. Since Brooke's drawing arm wasn't the broken one, Aly was sure she would be making tons of pictures while she was resting today.

"Joan," Aly said, "if it's okay with you, I'm going to call Brooke on the True Colors telephone. I promise not to tie up the line."

Aly took the cordless phone through the main salon into the Sparkle Spa, where she, Charlotte, Lily, and Sparkly plopped down on the big floor pillows in the drying and jewelry-making area. Sophie sat at one of the manicure stations and leaned back in the Teal Me the Truth–colored chair.

When Mom answered, she told Aly that Brooke was sleeping but would probably be up by the time Aly got home.

Aly hung up, a little sad that she hadn't gotten to talk to her sister.

"It's okay, Al," Charlotte said. "You'll see her after the Angels' pedicures. Oh, and Anjuli's manicure." Anjuli was the goalie and the only soccer player who needed sparkle power on her hands as well as her feet.

"Right," Aly answered, starting to feel panicky. According to her watch, the soccer girls would start arriving in two minutes, and she hadn't finished her homework yet, which meant she had already broken one of her mom's rules for the Sparkle Spa. She had a feeling that before the day was over, she would break some other rules, too. Eleven pedicures and one manicure all by herself was not going to be easy. Not even close.

Aly took a deep breath and pulled out a piece of paper and a glitter pen from the desk at the back of the room and started a new list.

<u>Other Ways All the Pedicures Could
Get Done</u>
1. A True Colors manicurist could
   help.
2. Sparkle Spa could be open
   tomorrow too, so I could polish
   fewer people each day.
3. Enlist a lot of helpers.

This was good! Aly had come up with great options!

"I'll be right back," she said to the girls as she ran out into the main salon.

"Joan!" she said "Joan! I have eleven girls coming in for pedicures and one who also needs a manicure, and it's just me because of Brooke's broken arm. I know it's only a kid salon, but is there any, any chance one of the True Colors manicurists could help? Just for a little while?"

Joan looked over at Aly, then looked down at the schedule in front of her and shook her head. "I really wish someone here could give you a hand, Al," she said. "But with your mom out, we're already all over-booked, taking care of her clients along with our own."

Aly felt like a balloon that had just been popped. But she understood.

"Okay," she said. "Thanks, Joan."

When Aly got back to the Sparkle Spa, Charlotte said, "What was that all about?"

Aly picked up her list again and crossed out the first option. "I'd thought of a way to get the pedicures done faster, but none of the grown-ups have time to help. Instead, maybe I'll see if some of the soccer girls can come tomorrow," she said, underlining the second item on her list.

"You can't," Lily said. "Remember? We have to do research for our Lewis and Clark project tomorrow after school."

Aly closed her eyes. She had totally forgotten about Lewis and Clark. That left her third and final option: *Enlist helpers.*

She walked over to the polish display wall and grabbed bottles of Strawberry Sunday, Under Watermelon, Lemon Aid, Orange You Pretty, and We the Purple—the colors for the rainbow sparkle pedicures. "In that case," Aly said, "I need someone to be a bottle opener and closer for me today."

"I'll do it," Charlotte said, raising her hand.

"And I can be in charge of the donations," Lily said, picking up the teal strawberry-shaped cookie jar the girls used to collect donations. "I'll make sure everyone contributes before they leave."

"How about Sophie, Aly? Do you have a job for her?" Charlotte asked.

Sophie was quietly painting her nails with Red Between the Lines, a newish color that looked kind of like a mixture of red and gray. She screwed the top back onto the bottle and held up her hands. "Can I be a second manicurist?" she asked.

Aly walked over and inspected Sophie's nails. She'd done a nice job. Not quite as professional as Aly's and Brooke's polishing, but better than most people's. "Whoa!" Aly said. "Good work."

"Brooke and I have been polishing each other's nails," Sophie told her. "It's not perfect yet, but maybe it's good enough to fill in for Brooke, since it's just you today?"

Aly looked at Sophie's hands again. A little polish was on the skin around both of her thumbnails, and she'd missed two spots on the corner of her right pinkie.

And another on the bottom of her left pointer finger. The polish on one of her ring fingers was a little gloppy too.

Aly sighed. "I'm not sure if you're ready yet, Soph," she said. "So first let's see how it goes with just me polishing."

Sophie looked at her own nails, inspecting them the way Aly had. "I see what you mean," she admitted. "I'll keep practicing. For now, I can help with nail drying and filling the pedicure basins. Is that okay?"

"Great," Aly said, and she and Sophie turned to fill the pedicure basins with water. But before she could even flip on the faucet, Jenica came into the Sparkle Spa with Valentina, one of the other soccer players.

"Happy Tuesday!" Valentina called.

Jenica glanced at Aly, Charlotte, Lily, and Sophie. "Actually, none of you look very happy," she said.

"Brooke broke her arm," Lily answered.

"Oh, man," Jenica said. "Tell her I'm sorry. I broke my wrist at summer camp once. I couldn't play sports or go swimming for six weeks after that."

"Wait a minute," Valentina said. "Aly, are you polishing all by yourself?"

"That's the plan," Aly said. "Why don't we get started?"

Two hours and twelve minutes later Aly had done eight pedicures and still had three to go . . . plus one manicure. She was running very, very late. Usually, the Sparkle Spa was closing about now. Her friends were being as helpful as possible, and the soccer girls were being as patient as possible, but Aly could tell they all wanted to get this over and done with. She was also pretty sure she had nail polish smeared all over her forehead—We the Purple, to be exact.

"Okay . . . next," Aly called out. "Sophie, could you please refill the pedicure basin on the right?"

Mia walked over and hopped into the chair. "I hope Brooke's ready to polish again before the dance showcase."

Aly felt the blood drain from her face. "That's *this* Friday?"

Mia nodded. Aly groaned. A group of the girls who attended Miss Lulu's dancing school were in a dance showcase, so they could show their families what they'd been working on all fall, and many of them had booked manicure appointments for Thursday after school.

"I don't mean to be mean or anything," Mia said,

"but unless Brooke is back or you have someone else doing nails, I might cancel my manicure appointment for the showcase. Giovanna and I have been waiting for half an hour for our rainbow sparkle pedicures. And we have homework. If it weren't for the quarter-finals, we'd have left by now."

Aly felt a headache coming on. "I'm really sorry," she said. "I think Brooke will be back by then. I promise the wait won't be as long on Thursday."

Mia nodded. "Okay. I really *do* want a manicure before the showcase. I want shiny nails to go with my shiny costume. We're dancing to a song called 'Stop! In the Name of Love,' and we have red leotards with white trim and white leg warmers—all covered with sequins and glitter."

"That sounds awesome," Charlotte said as she uncapped a bottle of clear polish. "And it's cool that you do soccer and dance."

"They're both fun," Mia said, easing her feet out of the warm pedicure water.

Just as Charlotte opened the Strawberry Sunday, Joan rushed into the Sparkle Spa. "The drain snake! The drain snake!" she yelled. "Aly, where's that twisted metal thing that snakes down the drain to clear out clogs?"

"I saw that before!" Lily said, hurrying to the back closet and retrieving a wiggly metal contraption. "Here!"

"Cookies for you," Joan told her. "I'll bake you a whole batch."

Joan's delicious cookies were famous all over town. Receiving an entire batch was one of the best presents ever.

"Running a salon by yourself isn't all it's cracked up to be, huh, Al?" Joan said before zipping back into True Colors.

Aly sighed. It was definitely better to run a salon as a team.

"Charlotte," she said, "ready with the polish?"

Charlotte nodded.

"Okay," Aly said, "here we go." But as she polished Mia's toes, she worried about what in the world she would do on Thursday if Brooke wasn't back at work by then. With fourteen dancers on the schedule, there was no way Aly could polish that many fingers alone.

thRee

We the Purple

The next thing Aly knew, Joan was saying, "Wake up, sleepyhead. You're home."

Aly barely remembered closing her eyes, let alone falling asleep on the ride to her house.

"That was some day, huh, Al?" Joan said.

Aly got out of the backseat of the car with Sparkly and walked over to Joan's window. "I don't know what I'm going to do if Brooke can't polish on Thursday," she told Joan. "Going to school all day and then spending so many hours at the salon is exhausting."

"I hear you," Joan said. "But Brooke and your mom might be out for the rest of the week, Aly. Both of us had better be prepared to be busy."

Aly's stomach fell. Brooke might be out the whole week? That couldn't be. Aly needed her there on Thursday. "Are you coming in?" she asked Joan.

"I think I need to go home and relax, just like you do. But please tell your mom to call me if she has time later. Stay strong, kiddo."

"You too," Aly said. "Thanks for the ride. I have to work on a Lewis and Clark project tomorrow, so I probably won't see you. But I'll stop by afterward if I can."

Joan nodded and scratched Sparkly behind the ears. "Give Brooke a hug for me."

"I will," Aly said, and then she and Sparkly started walking up the driveway.

By the time Aly reached the house, Mom was

there, opening the front door. "Brooke's sleeping again," she whispered, "so be quiet when you come in. Keep Sparkly quiet too."

Sleeping again? Aly couldn't believe it. "No problem," she whispered back, covering Sparkly's mouth with her hand. Aly walked in, put Sparkly down, and slipped off her shoes. She dropped her bag on the floor and fell into her mother's arms. "I'm so tired," she said. "And hungry. Going to school *and* going to work is hard!"

Over two tall glasses of milk, peanut butter and jelly sandwiches, and a plate of celery, Mom and Aly talked about both salons, Brooke's arm, and Dad's schedule.

"Joan said you might be home with Brooke all week," Aly said. "Is that true? Because I need her in the salon."

"I'm not sure," Mom said. "We'll have to see how she feels."

Aly nodded. She hoped Brooke would feel better super fast. But even if she didn't, Aly thought Mom should go back to True Colors to help Joan and the rest of the staff. "Why can't you call a babysitter or ask Dad to come home if someone needs to stay with Brooke?" she asked.

"I'd hate to leave Brooke with a sitter if she's not feeling well. And Dad's trying to change his plans," Mom answered, "but he's not sure he can. He'll definitely be home earlier than usual on Friday, though."

Aly nodded. Dad traveled a lot for work. He was usually gone from Monday afternoon until Friday afternoon. Sometimes he even got stuck places because of bad weather or bad airplanes or late meetings and got home on Saturday.

"So how did everything go at the salon?" Mom asked.

"Oh, Mom, it was crazy!" Aly said, leaning back in her chair. "I was the only one polishing in the Sparkle Spa, and I had to do eleven pedicures and one manicure, and my friends helped, but mostly, it was all up to me to get it done."

"That's what happens when you're the CEO of a business," Mom said, smiling a tiny bit.

"The what?" Aly asked. She had no idea what Mom was talking about.

"CEO," Mom said. "Chief executive officer. It's another name for the boss—the person who's in charge of everything at a company. Sometimes when you're the CEO, you have to jump in and take care of things—do more than you thought you would have to—because it's your business. You want it to succeed."

Aly nodded. That's how she'd felt this afternoon at the Sparkle Spa. She couldn't let the customers down. But then she thought about Joan running True Colors today and taking care of the clogged drain. "Are you the CEO of True Colors?" Aly asked her mom.

Mom nodded. "President and CEO is what my business card says."

"What about Joan? Does she have a title?"

"That's a good question," Mom said. She took a bite of celery and thought for a minute before she spoke. "Joan's my only senior manicurist, so she's second in command at the shop. When I'm not there, she takes over."

"Just senior manicurist?" Aly asked. "If she's in charge when you're not there, shouldn't she have a more important job title than that? One with initials, like yours?"

"You know, Aly," Mom said, "I think that's actually a very good idea. I've been thinking about hiring a COO, a chief operating officer. That person's job would be to manage the day-to-day organization of the salon. Then I can work more on getting new customers and maybe even starting a second shop. I'll talk to Joan about that."

"Joan watches Sparkly and bakes all the time and was great today at taking care of a broken pedicure basin, no problem," Aly said. "I bet she'd be a good COO. As long as she still gets to do manicures. I know she likes that part. Oh, and also—I just remembered: She said to call her tonight when you have time."

"Thanks for the message," Mom said. "I'll give her a call when we're finished with dinner."

"Are there other jobs?" Aly asked. "With initials like CEO and COO? For a business, I mean?"

Mom nodded. "Businesses can have a chief financial officer—"

"CFO?" Aly asked.

"Yes," Mom said, after swallowing a bite of sandwich. "And sometimes a chief marketing officer, a chief creative officer, a chief security officer, a chief digital officer, a chief legal officer . . . there are a lot. You can have someone in charge of every part of a business. Bigger companies have all those positions and more. Smaller companies sometimes just have a CEO."

Aly licked a drop of jelly off her thumb. "Will True Colors get all of those?"

"Maybe one day if I open lots and lots of salons and we need a team to run all of them."

"Is that what you want to do?" Aly asked. "Open lots of True Colors salons?" She hadn't known that was her mom's plan, but now it seemed like maybe it was.

"Just dreaming," Mom said. "I'm just dreaming. Far into the future. For now, we've got one salon and one broken arm to look after."

She pushed her empty plate forward. "Anyway, as the co-CEO of the Tanner household, I've made an EMD—an Executive Mother Decision." Mom grinned and continued: "Brooke has to rest and recuperate. I don't want the two of you jumping around. So I've moved some of your clothes and your sparkle pens and a few pieces of your favorite purple paper into the office upstairs. While Brooke's in pain, I think it's better for you to move in there. At least for a few days."

As Mom brought their dishes to the sink, she added. "And tomorrow, can you please pick up Brooke's homework assignments and any other schoolwork she'll miss?"

"Sure," Aly said, her brain quickly switching from True Colors to her sister. "But . . . what if Brooke needs someone in the middle of the night? I should be there to help her."

"I left the cordless phone with her," Mom said. "She'll call my cell if she needs something. Besides, if she doesn't feel well in the middle of the night, I don't want her to wake you. Don't forget, you have school tomorrow."

Aly was not happy. She didn't like the idea of sleeping in the tiny office. And she didn't like not being with Brooke, either.

"Can I at least go check on her?" Aly asked.

Mom nodded. "Just don't wake her if she's sleeping."

"I won't," Aly said.

She tiptoed up the steps and slowly pushed open their bedroom door. She poked her head in and saw Brooke, her arm wrapped in a big white cast, asleep in her bed. Sparkly was curled up at her feet. Her stuffed animals were next to her.

"Hi, Brooke," Aly whispered. But Brooke didn't budge. Aly sighed. Hopefully, Brooke would be up the next morning before Aly left for school. She'd see then if Brooke would be able to polish with a cast on. Because Aly really, really needed her to be ready to work in the salon by Thursday!

fouR
Traffic Coney Island

The next morning when Aly looked in on Brooke, she was still sleeping. Sparkly hadn't moved from the end of her bed. Her stuffed animals had fallen to the floor.

"She had a rough night," Mom said when Aly walked into the kitchen. "Her arm really hurt. I'm glad she finally fell back asleep."

Aly had not planned on this.

"But I need to know about the polishing!" she

cried. "We have *fourteen* manicures for the dance showcase tomorrow!"

Mom sighed. "I'm sorry, honey. But I wouldn't count on Brooke being able to help. Think about it, Al. Would you be able to polish with one arm in a cast or a sling?"

Aly hadn't really considered that. She held her left arm against her stomach and realized that, without it, she wouldn't be able to open any bottles, file fingernails, keep a customer's hand steady, or polish well at all.

She closed her eyes. What was she going to do tomorrow afternoon? Aly already knew she couldn't ask one of the True Colors manicurists to help. And there were no days available to reschedule anyone before the showcase because of her research project.

Aly popped a few banana slices into her mouth

and grabbed her backpack. She would have to think of something while she was at school.

During gym, while the rest of her class played volleyball, Aly tried and tried to come up with a plan, but other than finding kids who could polish as well as she and Brooke could to work at the salon, she couldn't come up with anything. And really, no other kids she knew could polish like she and Brooke could.

After the final bell rang, Aly went to the library to work with Charlotte and Lily on their Lewis and Clark project. Half of their fifth-grade class was in there with them, and Ms. Abbott, the librarian, was going from group to group helping everyone out. In between researching, Aly and Lily and Charlotte talked about Brooke's arm and the fact that she wouldn't be able to work tomorrow.

"I wish I were a better polisher," Charlotte said.

"I wish I could polish at all," Lily added. "But you remember what happened last time I tried?"

"Orange pinkie toe," Charlotte and Aly said together. Then the girls giggled, in spite of the seriousness of their conversation.

Aly knew she would have to find a solution that didn't involve Lily painting people's entire pinkie toes orange. Because that would absolutely not be good for business at the Sparkle Spa.

When the girls finished their research and Ms. Abbott had to close the library for the day, Aly decided to stop by True Colors quickly to see if Joan needed anything. With Mom gone, Aly knew it would be crazy at the salon. And sure enough, she was right.

"Oh, thank goodness you're here! Can you pitch in with the usual stuff?" Joan asked the moment Aly entered the salon.

"Absolutely!" Aly said. She quickly took care of the jobs she and Brooke usually did at True Colors—went to the bank to turn twenties into singles, organized the polish wall, and refilled the rhinestones at Carla's, Jamie's, and Joan's stations.

When that was all done, Aly sat down to take a breather with Mrs. Franklin, one of the girls' favorite regulars, who was under the nail dryers.

"Where's your sister?" Mrs. Franklin asked. "I brought a new photograph of Sadie I know she would love to see." Sadie was Mrs. Franklin's dog, a famous dog model—or, at least, she was a little bit famous. She was in magazines and was the official spokes-dog for the Paws for Love animal shelter in town. Brooke especially loved seeing pictures of Sadie dressed in silly outfits from her photo shoots.

"She broke her arm chasing Sparkly," Aly replied. "But I'll tell her that you have pictures."

"A broken arm!" Mrs. Franklin said. "Well, that's too bad. But I think I might have something more than pictures to cheer her up. Would you mind unzipping the side pocket on my purse?"

Aly did as she was asked, pulling out a gold pencil case and opening it to find paw print stickers inside.

"Why don't you take a couple of those for Brooke to put on her cast?" Mrs. Franklin suggested. "It's Sadie's autograph."

Aly smiled. Brooke would love the stickers. "Thanks so much, Mrs. Franklin."

Mrs. Franklin nodded. "Of course, dear. And please tell your sister I hope to see her back in the salon soon."

"I will," Aly said.

Aly noticed Joan putting some paper on a clipboard and attaching a pen to it with a ribbon. "What's that?" she asked.

"Lately, there have been so many walk-in customers, in addition to our regulars," Joan explained. "There just isn't enough room, with all these people crowding here. So I made a chart: name, cell phone number, time of arrival. I'll call people five minutes before we're ready for them so they can run other errands and not clog up the salon while they're waiting."

Aly glanced around at the customers in the waiting area. Most of them looked a little impatient, checking their phones or reading magazines. Joan was right. They could probably put the time to better use running errands rather than sitting around until a manicurist freed up.

"Nice plan," Aly said. "Do you think my mom will like it?"

Joan massaged her forehead. "If she doesn't, she can discontinue it when she's back. But as long as I'm in charge, we have to keep business—and people—moving."

Aly nodded. She'd never seen Joan so serious about something salon-related before. Usually, she was the fun one who made cookies and hosted pizza picnics while Mom took care of salon business.

"Sounds great," Aly said. Then she looked at the clock. She really should head home now and see how Brooke was doing, but then she spotted a familiar face poking through the front door.

"Sophie!" Aly said. "What are you doing here?"

"My mom is at the Sports Palace with my brother—buying him new sneakers. She said I could come here until they're done. I wanted to ask Joan how Brooke's doing."

"Big brother or little brother?" Aly asked.

"Big," Sophie said. "Sammy is at home with NaiNai." Sophie had two brothers, one in seventh grade and one who was three. Her grandma watched the three-year-old a lot. "I thought you had to work on Lewis and Clark today?"

"I did," Aly said. "But I stopped in here afterward for a little bit. I'm going to go home to see Brooke soon. My mom said she had a bad night, but I don't know how she's been today."

Sophie nodded. "Maybe I'll give her a call when I get home," she said.

Aly thought that was a good idea. "As long as she's not sleeping, I bet she'd like that."

Sophie nodded again, but she didn't leave the salon. "Um . . . ," she said. "Since you're here, there's something I wanted to show you." She held out her hand for Aly to see. "I practiced polishing a lot last night. Look."

Aly inspected Sophie's fingers. They were close to perfect. Not a drop of color on her skin, and every part of every nail was polished.

Aly grinned at Sophie. She really *did* need help tomorrow, and if Sophie could polish, that might fix Aly's scheduling problem. And even if she did a terrible job, the thing about polish is that it's easy to take off.

Aly looked at Joan's clipboard list. Then she took a big breath. "Sophie," she said, "I'm making an ESSD—an Executive Sparkle Spa Decision: You're now an official Sparkle Spa manicurist. Can you come in and polish tomorrow afternoon?"

Sophie beamed. "Absolutely!" she said.

For what seemed like the first time since Brooke broke her arm, Aly exhaled with relief. She put her arm around Sophie's shoulders. "Welcome to the team," she said.

"Aly!" Joan called from the reception desk. "Your mom is on the phone. She said you should head home now."

"I'll see you tomorrow," Sophie said, still smiling, and she walked out the door.

Aly got her backpack and started to head out too. But before she did, she stopped at the reception desk and blurted out, "Joan, just like you, I made a big decision today: I hired a new manicurist for the Sparkle Spa. Sophie. And now everything's going to be okay tomorrow."

At first Joan was silent. She stared at Aly for a few seconds, then finally said, "Aly, you're in charge of the Sparkle Spa. If you think that's the right thing to do, you should do it. But you have to take responsibility for this decision—no matter what happens."

Aly gulped. "I know," she answered. "I know."

five

White Christmas

When Aly walked through the door, Brooke was curled up on the overstuffed chair in the corner of the kitchen. Sparkly was at her feet.

"It feels like I haven't seen you in a *year*," Aly said, speeding over to her sister.

"More like three hundred years," Brooke answered. But she didn't sound like her usual bouncy self.

"Hi, Aly," Mom called from the laundry room. "I'll be up in a second!"

"She's transferring," Brooke said. "Washer to dryer."

Aly nodded. "So how does your arm feel?" she asked, studying Brooke's cast.

In the light it was really bright, like the White Christmas polish at the salon.

"It hurts," she said. Her face started to crumple. "And I can't polish nails. I can't go to school or to the Sparkle Spa. I never get to see anyone—not you or Joan or Sophie or anyone."

Aly sat on the arm of the chair and stroked her sister's head. She almost started crying herself because Brooke was so sad. This was definitely not the time to worry her with Sparkle Spa issues. Besides, Aly had fixed everything by hiring Sophie. She'd tell Brooke all about it later.

"You'll feel better soon," she said. "You'll go back to school and polish nails, and I'm here right now. I even brought your homework home. Besides, it's only been two days. Not even."

Brooke didn't stop complaining there, though.

"I didn't like the hospital either," Brooke said, snuggling her head against Aly. "It smelled funny. The doctor had to give me a shot, and I had to wait for a hundred million years. It was so boring . . . and a little scary."

"But you made it through," Aly said. "And you don't have to go back, right?"

"Wrong," Mom replied, coming up the steps into the kitchen. "You have a doctor's appointment in two weeks."

"When can everything get back to normal, Mom?" Brooke asked. "I can't wait."

"Remember what we talked about?" Mom answered. "Salon on Saturday. Your arm will feel much better by then. And school on Monday. You just need some time for the swelling to go down."

"That's too long," Brooke grumbled. "I *hate* having a broken arm."

Aly almost wanted to say, *Then you should've listened to me and not gone racing around the house after your hair band*, but she kept it zipped inside. Instead, she said, "I have a present for you. From Mrs. Franklin." Aly pulled the paw stickers out of her pocket.

Brooke smiled for the first time since Aly got home. "They're to decorate your cast."

Brooke looked at the fiberglass on her arm. "I can decorate it?" she asked.

Aly shrugged. "Mrs. Franklin seemed to think so."

"Mom," Brooke said, a little louder, "can I decorate my cast?"

"Sure," she said. "No reason why not. But after dinner."

"I'll cut your chicken tonight, Brookester. But don't get used to it," Aly offered, and gave her sister's braid a gentle tug.

After dinner, homework, and a quick conversation with Dad during which Aly begged him to come home— *now!*—Aly went back to the office to sleep on the couch, and Brooke got to stay up late decorating her cast.

Aly had unscrewed the tops of six different polishes—and had peeled up the edges of a bunch of stickers so it would be easier for Brooke with her one hand. But Aly wasn't allowed to stay up to help Brooke decorate.

Brooke had slept for so much of the day that she didn't have to go to bed yet. Plus, she could sleep in tomorrow because she wasn't going to school. A definite broken-arm perk, as far as Aly was concerned. One she was trying hard not to feel jealous about.

Aly got into bed, but she couldn't get comfortable. She couldn't stop thinking about all the dance show-case manicures scheduled for tomorrow. Sophie would be a good second manicurist, but Aly knew she'd be slow, slow, slow, just like Aly and Brooke had been at the beginning. She had to figure out a way to make the afternoon go as smoothly as possible.

Aly climbed out of bed and tiptoed over to her mother's desk. She quietly wiggled the mouse on the computer to see if it was on. The screen lit up.

On it were the words *Joan West, COO, True Colors*, along with the salon's address and phone number, plus a cool picture of a bottle of nail polish the same exact colors as the sign on the salon. It looked like the layout for a business card. Mom must have been working on it today. *Neat,* Aly thought.

She opened up a new document and started typing a list.

Ways to Speed Up Sophie's Polishing

1. Ask someone else to open and close bottles for her.

2. Have someone else or the customer remove any old polish.

3. Ask someone else to set up her station.

Lists always made Aly feel better and more prepared. Reading over it, she realized she'd added "someone else" to each item. If that "someone" wasn't Aly, who would it be?

Then the answer came to her. *Of course,* Aly thought, and typed:

4. Ask Charlotte and Lily if they'll also help.

With her mind a bit quieter now, she climbed back into bed. But just as she was about to fall asleep, Aly sat up with a start. *Oh no!* She never told Brooke—or Mom—about hiring Sophie. Or that their other friends had helped out on Tuesday.

Although she hadn't meant to keep it from Brooke, Aly also didn't want Brooke to feel bad about not being able to work at the salon this week, so maybe it was a good thing that she'd forgotten to tell her. Besides, Aly decided as she snuggled back into bed, Brooke wouldn't mind anyway. Charlotte and Lily had helped out in the Sparkle Spa before, and Sophie *was* her best friend after all.

Six

Copperfield

After school on Thursday, Aly, Sophie—*and* Charlotte and Lily—sped to True Colors. At some point they gave up racewalking and started running, so they were all a little out of breath by the time they ran through the salon's front door.

"Carrots are in the fridge!" Joan said as the girls rushed in. "Water, too."

Mom usually had snacks waiting for the girls when they arrived after school. Aly was happy that Joan had remembered. She was starving.

"Oh, and Lily, there's a bag of cookies with your name on it," Joan called after the girls.

Once they were all in the back, Aly read from the list she had written during lunch that she'd titled "Jobs":

Lily: Set up the manicure stations
Charlotte: Open and close polish
    bottles and help people chose colors
Sophie: Second manicurist

Lily asked, "*Sophie's* polishing?"

Aly nodded.

"High five!" Lily said, holding her palm out to Sophie. Sophie smiled and slapped it.

Charlotte was happy with her job too. But then she looked around, like she was searching for something. "Color of the Week!" she said. "What is it?"

Aly's eyes popped open. Choosing the Color of the Week was usually Brooke's job, but without her here, Aly had totally forgotten. "How about one of the new Presto Change-o shades?" she suggested. "Arnold, the delivery guy, brought them yesterday, and they look like two different colors, depending on how the light hits them. Do you want to pick one, Charlotte? They're on the bottom shelf of the display, on the right."

Charlotte picked Copperfield, the gold and red shade. "How about this?"

"That's good," Aly said, nervously looking around. "Did I miss anything else? The dancers will be here any second."

"Well," Lily said, sounding a little nervous herself, "you know how the Sparkle Spa has special treatments? Like the rainbow sparkle pedicure for the soccer team and the thumbs-up man-icure for guys?

Should you create something special for the dancers?"

Lily was right. But Brooke usually thought up those, too. "How about . . . ," Aly said. "How about . . ."

"How about a heart on the dancers' pinkies, painted in a different color?" Sophie offered. "That way, everyone can show the audience how much they love dancing."

Aly nodded. "Good plan, Soph," she said. "Let's call it . . . 'I Love Dancing'! So, Charlotte, everyone has to pick two colors if they want the special I Love Dancing manicure. And we need to get some of those tiny nail art brushes my mom keeps in the closet."

"Got it," Charlotte said.

"Okay, everyone. Now we're ready," Aly announced.

But Lily corrected her. "The donation jar!" she said. "Aly, you *always* forget the donation jar. I'll be in charge of that, too."

"It's all yours, Lil," she said. "And *no* walk-ins. Scheduled dancers only. Sophie's not as fast as I am yet, so any walk-ins will have to come back another day. No exceptions."

"Yes, boss," Charlotte said, and everyone started laughing.

Aly thought about how lucky she was to have such good friends. She might not even need Brooke this week with them around.

A few minutes later the first dancers arrived.

Sophie was definitely slow—Aly could finish almost two manicures in the time it took Sophie to do one—but she was good. She chatted with the customers and didn't seem nervous at all. She did mess up once, but luckily, it was on Mia—and since Mia was a regular and had gotten to know Sophie at the Sparkle Spa, she didn't mind so much.

"It's your first day on the job," Mia said to Sophie.

"Don't worry. You're doing better than *I* could ever do."

Aly was leading a girl named Maisy over to the drying station when Charlotte's twin brother, Caleb, peeked into the salon.

"Um," he said, "how's it going? Charlotte said you might need some help, and, well, I finished up at baseball practice in the park. Mom said it was okay if I came."

Aly grinned. Caleb was probably the nicest boy in the whole fifth grade. "I think we're okay," she said. "It's busy, but it's not that bad."

Caleb pointed at Lily. "What's going on over there?" he asked. She was organizing Sophie's manicure station with one arm while the other was hugging the big teal donation jar.

"She's doing two jobs—donations collector and station resetter," Aly explained.

Aly could barely hear Caleb when he spoke: "I

can do one of them, if you want. I mean, probably the donation jar, because I don't know about setting up, um, what did you call them? Stations?"

"Great idea," she said. Then she turned to Lily. "Caleb's going to help with the donations for a bit."

Lily darted over and handed him the ceramic strawberry. "Thanks," she said. "But just so you know, collecting donations is *my* favorite job, so I'm going to want it back."

Caleb scrunched his eyebrows. "Sure," he said. "No problem." Caleb parked himself and the giant strawberry by the Sparkle Spa door. "This way, I can do security, too, just like my dad," he said. Caleb and Charlotte's dad was chief of security for one of the largest buildings in town.

"I don't know if we need security," Aly told him, "but we do need someone to tell walk-ins that we're booked up." Aly handed Caleb the appointment book.

"All the dancers who are scheduled for a manicure are written down in here. Don't let anyone else in, okay?"

Aly was in the middle of an I Love Dancing manicure for a girl named Zorah, with Golden Delicious fingernails and Copperfield pinkie hearts, when she heard Caleb say, "I'm sorry. If you don't have an appointment, I can't let you in."

Aly stopped mid-polish. And groaned. It was Suzy Davis.

Ever since Aly fixed Suzy's messed-up manicure and hairdo before the Sixth-Grade Fall Ball a few weeks ago, Suzy had been nicer to her than she used to be. But Suzy was still Suzy. That meant she still had some mean inside her.

"I need a manicure. Now," Suzy demanded. "And it looks like Sparkle Spa is open today. So I'm coming in. It's a free country."

Caleb stood in the doorway. "Even in a free country, there are private places where people get to make their own rules. The rule here is that you need an appointment to come in. At least for today. No walk-ins." He looked over at Aly for confirmation.

"I'll be right back," Aly told Zorah. Usually, Brooke was the one who stood up to Suzy, but today Aly had no choice. She walked over to the door.

"What's the problem, Suzy?" she asked.

"I just cracked my thumbnail. I need a manicure. This minute." She shoved her broken nail past Caleb into Aly's face. Aly winced. It looked like it hurt.

"Suzy, I can't take care of that right now—we're too busy today with the dance showcase—but I can give you a nail file. You can fix the cracked part yourself."

"This is a nail salon," Suzy answered, her voice growing louder. "Not a do-it-yourself place. This is ridiculous!"

All of the dancers in the salon stared at Suzy.

Caleb cleared his throat. "If you don't leave, I'm going to get Joan."

"What is your *problem*?" Suzy said. "I mean, all I want is a manicure!"

Caleb didn't budge. "Bye, Suzy," he said.

Suzy glared at him. "You stink big-time, Caleb Cane," she huffed, and left.

Charlotte beamed. "Isn't my brother awesome?" she said.

"He sure is," Aly agreed, walking back to her station. "Zorah, let's finish up your fingers."

By five thirty Aly had done nine manicures and Sophie had done five. "Nice work, team! I couldn't have done this without you," Aly said. Even though she missed Brooke, she was super happy she'd gotten through the day without any major disasters. Well, not counting Suzy Davis, but truly, because of Caleb, that had been only a minor mishap.

And right then and there, Aly made the biggest ESSD of all: She offered everyone jobs at the Sparkle Spa.

Lily would be the CFO; Charlotte, the COO; Caleb, the chief of security; and Sophie, a manicurist.

Aly was delighted with her new Sparkle Spa team. She knew Brooke would be too. At least she hoped so.

Seven
Silversmith

Aly didn't have to wait long to find out how Brooke felt.

She arrived home to two surprises: a happy Dad, who had managed to return one day earlier and . . . a furious Brooke, who had just gotten off the phone with Sophie.

"Sophie is a Sparkle Spa manicurist? And she polished nails today instead of me? And you let Charlotte pick the Color of the Week? Who made you the boss of the world?" Brooke shouted. She stomped up the stairs and slammed the bedroom door.

Sparkly started yapping and whimpering.

Mom and Dad exchanged looks.

Aly felt her face turning the color of Ruby Red Slippers nail polish. It wasn't exactly the response she was expecting.

"Aly, sit down," Mom said firmly. "And, Mark, why don't you go check on Brooke?"

Sparkly followed Dad upstairs while Aly and her mother sat across from each other at the kitchen table.

"Is what Brooke said true?" Mom asked.

"I had no choice, Mom," Aly said. "Remember how you said that the CEO has to jump in and make decisions and take care of emergencies? Without Brooke and you around, I had to make sure the Sparkle Spa customers were taken care of."

Mom didn't answer, so Aly continued. "Isn't that what the leader of a business does, Mom?"

Her mother smiled. It was a small one, but it was a smile.

"You're right, Aly. That is what the person in charge has to do. But I think you may have forgotten that your sister is your partner. She works with you, not for you. She shouldn't have heard the news from Sophie. In fact, she should have been part of the decision."

Aly felt her stomach drop a little. She couldn't argue. Mom was right, and Aly had overlooked that point, but still, she thought her decisions were pretty good ones. "Everything happened so quickly," she started to explain. "And I didn't want Brooke to worry about not being around to help during such a busy week. I just wanted to do what was best—for our customers and for Sophie and Brooke and everyone.

Charlotte and Lily and Caleb helped out too. If they hadn't, it would've been a disaster at the Sparkle Spa, and we've worked so hard to build it. I didn't want it to fall apart just because of Brooke's arm."

Mom looked at Aly for a long moment. Then she got up and gave Aly a hug from behind, resting her chin on Aly's head. For a second Aly kind of wanted to cry. "Why don't you wait until Dad comes downstairs, and then you can apologize to your sister," Mom finally said.

"I will," Aly told her. She knew she had to. She knew it was the right thing to do—plus, she hated it when Brooke was mad at her. But she knew that in addition to apologizing, she was going to have to tell her sister about giving the other kids jobs at the Sparkle Spa too. If Brooke was already upset about them working there for a day, she was *not* going to be happy about the longer-term arrangement. "First, I'm going to make a peace offering, though." Aly thought making Brooke's favorite snack might help out a little. It was worth a try.

As Aly made a heart-shaped cream cheese and jelly sandwich for Brooke, she and her mom talked about the new Presto Change-o colors that had arrived while Mom was home with Brooke—how some shades looked muddy, but how the metallics, like Silversmith, seemed popular.

When Dad came back into the kitchen, Aly quickly took the sandwich and a glass of chocolate milk upstairs. "Brooke?" she called, knocking on their bedroom door. "Brookester?"

"I'm not talking to you," Brooke answered.

"You just did," Aly said. "And I'm sorry. I'm so sorry. And I'm leaving you a present."

Then Aly went to the office—she figured it would take Brooke a little while to come around, and she still had some reading to do for her Lewis and Clark project. Once she was finished sticking flags on the book Ms. Abbott had given her about Sacagawea, noting that Lewis and Clark would probably have gotten lost and not been very good explorers without Sacagawea's help, Aly sat down at the computer. After clicking around for a bit, she found the new business card Mom had made for Joan. She copied it and pasted it into a new document over and over, then started typing new wording into each little rectangle. In just a few minutes she'd made Sparkle Spa business cards for everyone on the team—Sophie, Lily, Charlotte, Caleb, and herself—so she could give them out tomorrow at school. She pressed print and watched the pages pile up.

She'd have to cut the thick paper to the right size, but the cards looked pretty good. She especially liked the purple star she'd added in place of the polish bottle Mom had on Joan's card. It had little lines around it to make it look like it really was sparkling. Once Brooke was talking to her again for real, she'd make one for Brooke, too.

Aly picked up the sheets of paper.

"What are those?" Brooke said, standing at the door.

Aly jumped and the pages went flying. "You scared me!" she said. Aly bent down to pick up the papers. "They're Sparkle Spa business cards."

Brooke adjusted the strap of the sling on her shoulder. "For us?" she asked, her eyes growing big. "Is that another way besides the sandwich that you're apologizing to me? Because that's so cool!"

"Well, they're Sparkle Spa business cards, but they're not just for us." Aly swallowed hard. She knew she had to say it, but the words stuck in her throat. "They are for our friends," she finally continued. "Sophie wasn't the only one who helped out. Charlotte, Lily, and Caleb worked there today too, so I gave them all jobs at Sparkle Spa."

Brooke blinked once. Then twice. Aly was afraid Brooke would cry. But she didn't. She yelled. "You did *what*?"

"They're our friends. And I needed help. Fourteen dancers were booked, and there was no way I could give them manicures all by myself." Aly was trying to defend herself, but it sounded like a bad excuse, even to her.

Tears ran down Brooke's face. "Sparkle Spa is *our* thing, Aly. *Ours.* And you're acting like it's only *yours*," she sniffed.

"You left me, Brooke!" Aly said. "You left me all alone, and I had to do everything myself. We're lucky our friends offered to help; otherwise, I would've had to cancel everything. All the girls who were counting on us for manicures for their showcase would've been so upset. That would have been terrible for Sparkle Spa business."

Brooke crossed her unbroken arm over her broken one. "You could've talked to me about it. It's like you didn't even care I wasn't there. Did you at least give me a good job on my business card?" Brooke asked, her voice quivering.

"I didn't give you one yet," Aly muttered. "But you can choose your own. Right now Lily's in charge of money, and Charlotte's in charge of the schedules and how things work, and Sophie only wanted to be a manicurist, not in charge of any—"

"What about you?" Brooke asked.

"Um, I'm . . . I'm CEO," Aly whispered.

"What does that mean?" Brooke demanded.

"Well, it kind of means I'm in charge of everything," she admitted. But then she quickly added,

"But we can share the title. Or—or you can have it if you want it, and I can be something else."

Brooke started crying now for real. "You didn't even think about me! I broke my arm, and you forgot all about me and took away the Sparkle Spa. I don't even want to be your sister anymore." She ran out of the office, down the hall.

And before Brooke slammed the bedroom door for the second time that night, she yelled out, "And don't worry about giving me a job, Aly. I quit."

eight
Blue Skies

Friday was usually one of Aly Tanner's favorite days of the week: No school for two whole days, Sparkle Spa for one full day each weekend (not just a weekday afternoon), and she and Brooke always polished each other's fingernails first thing on Saturday morning so they would look fancy all weekend long.

But this Friday, Aly floated through the day, barely talking to anyone or noticing anything. She gave Charlotte, Lily, Caleb, and Sophie their new business cards, and she wished the dancers luck for their showcase that night, and she stopped by True Colors right after school to see if Joan needed any help, but the whole time, she was thinking about Brooke and how she'd quit their whole Sparkle Spa business. No matter how many lists Aly tried to make, she couldn't figure out a way to fix things.

When Aly got home, Brooke was sitting in the overstuffed chair in the kitchen reading *Tales of a Fourth Grade Nothing*. She didn't even look up when Aly walked in.

Mom and Dad were busy preparing dinner and didn't seem to notice that the sisters weren't on speaking terms. Aly knew she could ask her parents for advice, but she wanted to try to fix the problem herself.

After a quiet dinner, Aly went to the office, took out a sparkly pen and a piece of purple paper, and started to write.

Dear Brooke,

Please come back to the Sparkle Spa.

It won't be the same without you.

You are my sister, and we started the spa together. I should have thought of that before anything else.

No one can ever take your place.

I'm so, so sorry.

Love, your sorry sister,

Aly

Aly slipped the note under their bedroom door, along with a Sparkle Spa business card that she'd made for Brooke that named her co-CEO. Aly realized that she should have given Brooke that title from the start. The sisters were a team, and she'd never forget that again. If only Brooke would agree to come back to the Sparkle Spa. . . .

* * * * *

Early Saturday morning Aly was awakened by Sparkly's lick, followed by a hug—a hug from Brooke.

"I forgive you, Aly," Brooke whispered in her sister's ear. "Let's get ready for work."

Brooke needed help getting her cast through the armhole of her T-shirt. And with the straps on her sandals. And with brushing her hair, too. Aly even put toothpaste on Brooke's toothbrush for her—but she drew the line when Brooke asked if Aly would brush her teeth for her. So Brooke did that herself.

"Broken arms are the pits," Brooke said, after she spit out her toothpaste.

Aly nodded. "But you'll be better soon."

"Six weeks!" Brooke answered as she handed her hair elastic to Aly. "That's forever."

"Not even close to forever," Aly said.

✳   ✳   ✳   ✳   ✳

An hour later Mom was driving the girls to the salon. Sparkly was spending the day with Dad.

"The whole team will be there today," Aly warned Brooke.

"I know, I know," Brooke said. "It's fine. I'm glad they helped keep the Sparkle Spa in business."

When the girls walked through the front door of True Colors, all of the manicurists made a big deal over Brooke being back. Each one wanted to sign and decorate her cast. Meanwhile, Aly headed to the Sparkle Spa, where she was surprised to see Charlotte, Caleb, and Lily already there. Sophie was there too, sitting at the second manicure station, ready for work.

"Look what I did," Charlotte said as soon as Aly walked in. She pointed to three sheets of paper attached to the wall in a row, with a pen dangling from a string taped next to each sheet. Charlotte had made photocopies of the pages from the Sparkle Spa appointment book for next Tuesday, Friday, and Sunday.

"This way," she said, "customers can sign up for appointments themselves while they wait."

"Oh." Aly said. She sort of wished Charlotte had asked her first, and she was a little worried about what Brooke would think.

But before she could respond, Charlotte added, "And I made these signs for the front window of True Colors." She held up one that read: KIDS, COME TO THE BACK! SPARKLE SPA IS OPEN! And another that said: SPARKLE SPA IS CLOSED, BUT CALL TO MAKE AN APPOINTMENT. She'd left space underneath to include a phone number.

"I think we should get a business cell phone so people can leave messages," Caleb said.

"No cell phones allowed," Aly said quickly. "But thanks for thinking of it." She was starting to feel a tiny bit uncomfortable about all these new suggestions.

"And, Aly, look at the new donation box," Lily said. "The old jar could break, so I brought in this safe, which even has a combination lock." Lily practically shoved the box in Aly's face.

"Oh," Aly said again. She didn't want a new donation box. She loved the sparkly teal strawberry Mom had made in art school. And she knew Brooke did too. But what could she say? Lily was only trying to do her job as CFO.

A few seconds later Brooke walked in, her cast covered with rainbows and hearts.

"Brooke!" Sophie squealed, standing up. "I'm so glad you're back!"

Brooke squinted at her. "What are *you* doing in *my* manicure chair?" Brooke hissed.

Sophie's face paled. "I, um, I'm a manicur-ist now, remember? This is where I was sitting on Thursday . . . ," she said quietly.

Brooke looked around. "What's that on the wall? And why isn't the strawberry donation jar on the side table?" she said, clearly growing more upset at each new change she noticed.

"Charlotte made us sign-up charts, since she's the COO now," Aly said nervously. "What do you think?"

Brooke didn't answer. Instead, she focused on Caleb. "He won't be here all the time, will he? Everything will be different if there's a *boy* in the Sparkle Spa! Aly, you're ruining everything! Again!" She turned around and ran back into True Colors.

Aly's stomach flip-flopped. "I'm really sorry, everyone," she said. "I think Brooke is just a little surprised. It's my fault. I should've explained things better to her. I'll go get her."

But before Aly had a chance to follow her sister, two sixth graders from their school, Uma and Aubrey, came in for manicures and pedicures. Aly had totally forgotten about them, but they'd made appointments on Monday and were right there in the book. Aly poked her head into True Colors and saw Brooke talking to their mom.

"I picked my colors," Uma called out.

"Me too," said Aubrey. "Which are we doing first? Fingers or toes?"

Aly looked at Brooke one more time and then sighed. "Toes," she said to Aubrey and Uma. "Let's get started."

The day was busy with both regulars and walk-ins. Sophie was improving, but she was still pretty slow.

Charlotte kept coming up with new ideas every hour, from where to move the stations to what colors to paint the walls. Caleb pretty much sat near the door, checking out his sneakers. And Lily kept counting the donations over and over. Nobody asked about Brooke at all. But Aly was thinking about her all day long. She couldn't believe no one else was.

Even without Brooke, everything was going along smoothly. Aly was putting the top coat on Keisha's fingers—she was a second grader Aly knew from the library—when Charlotte said, "Aly, I think we should have two Colors of the Week, not just one. And three on special occasions like Halloween and the Fourth of July."

And that's when Aly snapped.

She waited until Keisha left and there were no customers in the salon. Then she exploded. "Charlotte, you have to stop asking me so many questions about colors and appointments. Lily, please stop rattling the coins in the box. And, Caleb, you haven't gotten off that chair all day!"

They all just stared at Aly.

No one said anything for close to a minute.

"Are you feeling okay?" Charlotte finally asked. "Did we do something wrong? We're just trying to be helpful."

Oh, boy. What had she done? Aly felt terrible. Really terrible. "No, it's me. Not any of you. I'm so sorry," she said. "I think I just miss Brooke."

Aly absolutely needed all her friends' help, but she *really* missed Brooke.

She missed their Secret Sister Eye Messages and Brooke pushing up her glasses and tugging her braid. She missed Brooke's awesome ideas. She missed Brooke's color combinations and the way she knew which new polish everyone would like best.

And if she was being perfectly honest, Aly had to admit that having all these new job titles at the Sparkle Spa had kind of added a few too many bosses to the mix. Did she *have* to accept every single one of their suggested changes now that Charlotte, Lily, Sophie, and Caleb were part of the team?

Being CEO was hard. And without Brooke, it was even harder.

The rest of the afternoon was fine, and the only one who seemed bothered by Aly's outburst was Aly. She made sure she was extra nice to everyone because of it, even though she hated the safe that Lily had brought and liked the manicure and pedicure stations exactly where they were.

"Thanks, everyone," Aly said as her friends were getting ready to leave. "Really. You all did a super job, and I'm sorry again for getting upset earlier."

"No problem, Aly. We know you miss Brooke. See you at school on Monday," Charlotte said, waving good-bye.

Sophie was the last to leave the spa. "I'm sorry I'm so slow, Aly, but I really love being here and polishing nails," she said quietly. "I just . . . I just wanted you to know that."

"Sophie, you're a great manicurist." Aly sighed. "I didn't mean to be mean today."

Once the Sparkle Spa was empty, Aly went on a hunt for Brooke. She found her sitting with Mom on the sky-blue bench in front of True Colors. They were both eating ice cream. With sprinkles. Aly didn't say a word, she just stood there listening.

Brooke was chattering away, too busy to notice her sister. "They changed things," she said. "While I was gone, Sophie took my spot and Charlotte made new signs and Caleb is a boy."

"Joan had new ideas too," Mom said. "For True Colors. I wish she would have asked me first, but sometimes being part of a team means letting other people do what they want to make a project or a game or a business the best it can be."

"I don't know if our friends love Sparkle Spa as much as I do," Brooke said, staring at the roses that Joan had drawn on her cast.

"You might be surprised, Brookie," Mom said. "They're just trying hard to make it even better than it already is."

"I guess," Brooke said. "But I liked it better when the team was just me and Aly, and we did everything together, just us."

Aly took a deep breath and finally spoke up. "I liked it that way too, Brooke." Then she sent a Secret Sister Eye Message that said, *I miss you so much.*

And when Aly felt tears forming in her eyes, she saw them in Brooke's eyes too.

nine

Forget Me Not

All day Sunday, Aly and Brooke talked about what had gone right and what had gone wrong after Brooke's accident. That way they could learn from what had happened.

They each made a list.

How to Fix Aly's Mistakes
1. Talk to Brooke before you make any Executive Sparkle Spa Decisions! She's your partner.

2. ESSDs should sometimes be discussed with Mom.

3. Think before you make big decisions, like hiring all your friends to work.

4. Don't yell at your friends in the Sparkle Spa. They're just trying to help.

5. Try not to be mean like Suzy Davis.

How to Fix Brooke's Mistakes

1. Watch out for backpacks that are lying on the floor.

2. Don't chase Sparkly through the whole entirehouse.

3. Don't get mad at Caleb for being a boy.

4. Sometimes it's okay when there are changes at the Sparkle Spa. People are just trying to make it even better.

5. Try not to be mean like Suzy Davis.

And when Charlotte, Lily, Sophie, and Caleb showed up for work at the Sparkle Spa on Tuesday, Aly folded up her list, stuck it in her back pocket, and apologized to them. She apologized again for her outburst on Saturday. She apologized for giving them all jobs without talking to Brooke first. And she told them that they could keep their jobs at the Sparkle Spa for as long as they wanted, but they had to understand that Brooke and Aly were the ones in charge. And they would make decisions together, just like Lewis and Clark. Even though those explorers needed help from their friends too, like Sacagawea.

"We know you're in charge," Charlotte said. "But we do love being here. We just want the Sparkle Spa to be the best kids' salon in the world."

"Yeah, it's been okay, but just so you know, I don't think I can hang out here all the time. I've got sports, too, you know," Caleb said.

Aly nodded and looked at Brooke, who was biting her lip to keep from smiling. Then Caleb took his post by the door, and the girls started to get ready for the Auden Angels' rainbow sparkle pedicures. Since Brooke couldn't polish, she decided her job was going to be standing near the polish display and talking to people. It really was the perfect job for her.

When the pedicures were done, all the players lined up to decorate Brooke's cast. Jenica grabbed a bottle of bluish-purple Forget Me Not polish. "Quickly," she said as she dipped the brush in and painted a star on Brooke's cast. "Because we have to get down to the field for practice for the semifinals on Saturday. You're coming to cheer us on, right? Rainbow sparkle power helped us get there."

"We'll be there," Aly said.

"Wouldn't miss it," Brooke added.

Lily and Charlotte nodded in agreement.

Caleb did too.

After the team left, Lily started counting the day's proceeds in the teal donation jar. The first thing Aly and Brooke had decided as co-CEOs was that the safe was out and the strawberry-shaped jar was back in. Their mom had made it after all, which made it extra special.

Lily handed Caleb a stack of bills and a handful of change. "Can you remember thirty-three?" she asked him.

He nodded.

Lily counted out some more money and handed that to Caleb too. Then she stood up.

"Ahem," she said. "This week the Sparkle Spa made exactly one hundred and seven dollars and—what was the number I told you, Caleb?"

"Thirty-three," he said.

"Thirty-three cents!" Lily finished. "That means it's time to contribute to a charity, right? Whichever one you choose?"

"Yep, every hundred dollars, we donate," Brooke confirmed.

Charlotte and Brooke had just finished organizing the polish wall and sat down on the floor near Caleb and Lily. "So are you guys going to pick a place to give the money to now?" Charlotte asked the sisters.

"We should," Aly said, turning to Brooke.

She saw Brooke looking around at Charlotte's sign-up sheets, which Aly and Brooke had decided could stay. And then her eyes traveled to Sophie, who'd made it possible for Sparkle Spa to stay up and running while her arm was healing.

Finally, Brooke looked at Aly and gave her a Secret Sister Eye Message: *Let's make it a team decision.*

Aly nodded in agreement, so Brooke asked, "What do you guys think?"

Everyone thought for a while.

"Puppies?" Charlotte suggested.

Aly glanced at Brooke, who shook her head.

"Great idea," Aly said, "but we already donated to the animal shelter."

"Dancers?" Sophie asked.

"Are they a charity?" Lily said.

"No, I guess not," Sophie agreed.

Then Brooke jumped up. "I know!" she said. "We should donate to kids who are in the hospital's emergency room—especially in the waiting area. It's so boring there and sometimes scary. The hospital can use the money to make a library, maybe—or at least some magazines and comic books to start. And then maybe people from all over town can donate books they don't want anymore. We'll tell Mrs. Bass that we'll take any of her sons' books that we can get!"

"I like that idea a lot," Aly told Brooke, beaming. Then she whispered in her sister's ear, *"But should we let everyone vote?"*

When Brooke nodded, Aly said, "Everyone who agrees with this choice, raise your hand."

Everyone raised their hand.

"Nice teamwork," she said with a smile.

Aly knew that for as long as she and Brooke needed them, Lily, Charlotte, Sophie, and Caleb would be there to help. But she and Brooke would still be in charge, just the two of them. Because that's how they liked it best.

ten

Diamond Jubilee

"May I have another slice, Joanie?" Brooke asked. "This pizza is delicious!" Her arm may have been in a cast, but that didn't stop Brooke from eating three slices of extra-cheese pizza.

True Colors and the Sparkle Spa were celebrating Joan's promotion to COO with a pizza party. She worked so hard and could always be counted on—and she came up with some great ideas while Mom was gone, proving that she had a good head for business. No one deserved this promotion more than Joan, Aly knew. She was so happy for her.

"Come on, Brooke. We'll be late for the game," Sophie said. Aly and Brooke had agreed that they should invite all their friends to Joan's party too, since they were part of the salon team now. "I don't want to miss kickoff."

"Okay, okay. One more bite and we'll all go," Brooke answered.

"Run, Jenica, run!" Brooke yelled.

"Get it to the goal!" Aly shouted.

"Kick it!" Lily screamed, jumping up and down.

"She's *fast*!" Caleb said.

Aly couldn't believe how quickly Jenica was moving as she bolted down the field. She was faster than anyone—and her hair was flying all over the place as she ran. The other girls were coming up behind her in different spots on the grass.

It was cool to see how the whole team worked together and knew how to play the different positions.

Jenica passed the ball to Bethany, who kicked it to Mia.

Aly watched Mia's Diamond Jubilee fingernails flash in the sun, with little Silversmith hearts on her pinkies. Sophie had polished her nails for the dance showcase over a week ago, and they were still holding up. "Your manicure's looking good out there, Soph," she said.

Sophie smiled.

Mia kicked the ball toward the goal, but a girl from the other team blocked the shot and sent it in the other direction. Bethany got there first, then kicked it. *Hard.* The ball went *flying, flying, flying* past the goalie's hands, right into the top left corner of the net.

GOAL!

The Angels won their semifinal match! The team ran cheering onto the field.

Aly heard Jenica scream, "We did it! We did it together!"

I wonder if rainbow sparkle power really did help them at all, Aly thought.

Brooke cheered. "They're a team, just like us," she said.

And that's exactly how Aly felt about the new crew at the Sparkle Spa. It hadn't been easy, but they'd done it together.

"So," Brooke said to Aly, Lily, Charlotte, and Caleb, after they'd congratulated all the Angels, "I heard the soccer girls are celebrating with ice cream. I think we should celebrate too. Not just because they won the game, but because we're a great team, just like them."

Aly smiled and threw her arm around her sister. "That," she said, "is one of your best ideas yet."

How to Give Yourself (or a Friend!)
an I Love Dancing Pedicure
By Aly (and Brooke!)

※ · ※ · ※ · ※ · ※ · ※

What you need:

Paper towels

Polish remover

Clear polish

One color polish for the base

(we suggest silver)

One color polish for the hearts

(we suggest copper)

Toothpicks

What you do:

1. Put some paper towels down on the floor so if anything spills, no one will get mad at you. (This

is very important. This one time we got Tickled Pink on our grandma's white rug. She was not happy at all.)

2. Rip off another paper towel, fold it up, and put some polish remover on it. If you have polish on your toes already, make sure you get it all off. If you don't, just rub the remover over your nails once to remove any dirt that might be on them. (Dirt makes polish look lumpy, and that is the absolute pits! No one wants lumpy polish!)

3. Rip off two more paper towels. Twist the first one into a long tube and weave it back and forth between your toes to separate them a little bit. (This will help keep polish off the skin of one toe when you're painting the one next to it.) Then do the same thing with the second paper towel on your other foot.

You might need to tuck the end of the paper towel under your pinkie toe if it pops up and gets in your way while you polish. (You can also use tape if you need to—but you probably won't need to.)

4. Open your bottle of clear polish and apply a coat on each nail. Then close the clear bottle up tight. (You can go in whatever order you want, but our favorite is big toe to pinkie on your right foot, then big toe to pinkie on your left foot. It's easy to keep track that way. But whatever you do, make sure you get them all!)

5. Open the silver polish (or whichever color you chose for your base; we like metallics for this pedicure). Apply one coat on all toenails. Close the bottle up tight.

6. Fan your toes to dry them a little, then repeat the fifth step. (If you don't do a second coat, the polish won't look as bright. Some people like to do a third coat, but we think that's too many. Plus then it takes even longer to dry.)

7. Fan your toes a little again. (You should actually fan them for more than a little while. We recommend singing the whole alphabet song three times in a row. Aly likes to show off and sing it backward, but I do it forward, and that's just fine.)

8. Open your copper polish (or whatever accent color you chose). Wipe the brush on the sides of the nail polish bottle and then balance the brush upside down so the polish doesn't drip anywhere.

Dip a toothpick into the polish and use it like a tiny paintbrush to draw a heart. (You will probably need to dip a few times to get the whole heart drawn.) Then repeat on the other pinkie toe. (Your pinkie toenail is smaller than your pinkie fingernail, so you may want to switch and put the heart on your big toe instead. Either way, it looks beautiful.) When you're done, close the bottle up tight.

9. Fan your toes again (one alphabet song should do the trick—forward or backward, it's up to you) and then open your clear polish. Apply a top coat of clear polish on all your toenails. Close the bottle up tight.

Now your toes have to dry. You can fan them for a long time (like, at least fifteen alphabet songs), or you can sit and make a bracelet or read a book or watch TV or talk to your friend until they're all dry. Usually, it takes about twenty minutes, but it could take longer. (After twenty minutes you should check the dryness by really carefully touching the nail of your big toe very lightly with your fingertip. If it still feels sticky, keep waiting! Patience is the most important thing—otherwise, you might smudge your pedicure and have to take it all off and do it all over again, which, let me tell you, is a very grumpy-making process. This one time that happened to me twice in a row, and I was ready to pull my braid out of my head, I was so mad about it!)

And now you should have a beautiful I Love Dancing pedicure! Even after the polish is dry, you probably shouldn't wear socks or closed-toe shoes for a while. (And make sure no one steps on your feet—not even your dog!) Bare feet or sandals are best so all your hard work doesn't get smooshed. (Besides, then you can show off your beautiful toes!)

Happy polishing!